MW01103238

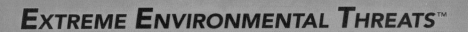

EXTREME ENVIRONMENTAL THREATS™

DESTRUCTION OF EARTH'S RESOURCES

The Need for Sustainable Development

Adam Winters

The Rosen Publishing Group, Inc., New York

To Jesse L., who was a good environmental citizen

Published in 2007 by The Rosen Publishing Group, Inc.
29 East 21st Street, New York, NY 10010

Copyright © 2007 by The Rosen Publishing Group, Inc.

First Edition

Library of Congress Cataloging-in-Publication Data

Winters, Adam.
Destruction of earth's resources: the need for sustainable development/by Adam Winters.—1st ed.
    p. cm.—(Extreme environmental threats)
Includes bibliographical references and index.
ISBN 1-4042-0746-5 (library binding)
1. Sustainable development—Juvenile literature. 2. Economic development—Environmental aspects—Juvenile literature. 3. Environmental policy—Juvenile literature. 4. Natural resources—Management—Juvenile literature.
5. Conservation of natural resources—Juvenile literature. I. Title. II. Series.
HC79.E5W565 2007
338.9'27—dc22
                                                                2005034189

Manufactured in the United States of America

On the cover: In the Philippines' capital of Manila, a young boy paddles a Styrofoam board along the polluted Maricaban River, which runs through one of the city's many slums. **Title page:** Nombaso Namba stands at the entrance to her home, made from waste materials collected at a nearby garbage dump, in the Etipini township, near Umtata, South Africa.

Contents

INTRODUCTION 4

1 PEOPLE 10

2 LAND 21

3 WATER AND AIR 32

4 ENERGY 43

GLOSSARY 56

FOR MORE INFORMATION 58

FOR FURTHER READING 60

BIBLIOGRAPHY 61

INDEX 62

Modern apartment buildings rise above the neighboring slum of Dharavi, in Mumbai, which was formerly known as Bombay, India.

The idea of sustainable development grew out of various environmental concerns that began to emerge in the 1960s and 1970s. To "sustain" is to be able to provide basic necessities or nourishment. "Development" refers to growth. By the late '60s, scientists and environmental groups were becoming worried about the destructive changes taking place on the earth. Human growth and development had resulted in an increase in wealth, technology, and production of food and manufactured goods, as well as the growth

of cities. At the same time, the world population was exploding, especially in some of the poorest "developing countries" of Africa, Latin America, and parts of Asia. New diseases were emerging. Air, water, and land pollution were on the rise. Moreover, the harmful effects of unrestricted industrial, farming, and fishing activities were threatening many precious plant and animal species. To address these concerns for the first time, the United Nations Conference on the Human Environment met in 1972 in Stockholm, Sweden. It wasn't until 1987, however, at the United Nations World Commission on Environment and Development, that the term "sustainable development" was defined by the Bruntland Commission as: "Development that meets the needs of the present without compromising [affecting] the ability of future generations to meet their own needs." In other words, sustainable development related to humans trying to achieve environmental, economic, and social progress while protecting natural resources essential to future life. Yet, when they looked around at the many problems facing the earth, many scientists and activists feared that a great deal of the development taking place was not at all sustainable. If governments, businesses, and citizens around the world did not change their ways, much of the planet, and eventually the population, would be destroyed. Sustainable development became an issue that urgently needed to be addressed.

The 1992 United Nations Conference on Environment and Development in Rio de Janeiro, Brazil, placed the topic of sustainability in the global spotlight. Close to 17,000 leaders and representatives from 178 nations, as well as 10,000 journalists from around the world, participated in this first "Earth Summit." Research was shared, reports were given, and many international agreements were made. Government and business leaders promised to take steps to reduce severe problems such as pollution and increase supplies of clean water to city dwellers.

The summit's findings and agreements were published in a general plan of action called Agenda 21. Based on the objectives outlined in this plan, leaders were to return home and create development strategies that would address specific problems in their own countries.

Unfortunately, despite increasing awareness and the creation of some useful projects, the next ten years saw a general rise in poverty, global inequality, and environmental destruction. Despite good intentions, it seemed that sustainable development was not a priority for either rich or poor nations. In part, many governments believed—mistakenly—that sustainability was expensive and would be an obstacle to development. Business leaders and politicians alike worried that strict rules protecting the environment would limit economic growth. People felt that poverty and health issues were more urgent than preserving nature. Moreover, numerous leaders of developing countries thought that the wealthier nations, which use more energy and create more pollution, should be shouldering additional costs and taking extra responsibility for protecting the environment.

With these setbacks in mind, in 2002, over 20,000 world government and business leaders as well as scientists, environmentalists, and other concerned specialists met for another Earth Summit in Johannesburg, South Africa. World leaders agreed upon certain wide-ranging international targets and deadlines. For instance, they set a goal to decrease by half the number of people without access to basic sanitation by 2015. This time, however, participants were determined to place emphasis on specific projects and actions that would truly make a difference. Instead of sweeping declarations and goals that, in practice, would not be carried out, they concentrated their efforts on smaller and more focused plans. Many projects involved adopting a series of practical, ongoing measures that would directly improve people's lives in specific communities and regions. Such plans encouraged cooperation between governments, businesses, private groups, and organizations. Citizens themselves would carry out the plans at local levels.

In March 2005, the United Nations released a massive study known as the Millennium Ecosystem Assessment. It had taken four years and the aid of over 1,300 researchers from 95 nations to draw up this 2,500-page report. It included the following conclusions about the state of the earth and the possibility of sustainable development:

Everyone in the world relies on natural ecosystems to provide the conditions for a decent and healthy life.

In recent decades, in order to meet growing demands for food, fresh water, and energy, humans have dramatically harmed these ecosystems.

While billions of lives have improved, human activity has weakened nature's capacity to provide essential services such as purification of air and water, protection from disasters, and supply of natural medicines. Meanwhile, the very real possibility that thousands of species will become extinct further threatens our own well-being.

Today's knowledge and technology can help reduce our negative impact on ecosystems. However, such knowledge will not be fully used until we stop thinking of nature as free and everlasting and recognize both its preciousness and its limitations.

This book will explore some of the greatest problems that threaten our ecosystems and our own lives. It will also look at some of the solutions that could help transform sustainable development from a series of ideas into a new way of living that benefits the planet and all of its inhabitants.

A young boy plays in the polluted waters of Indonesia's capital, Jakarta.

The world population has grown more in the last fifty years than it has throughout all of human history. Currently, there are an estimated 6 billion people living on Earth. And according to a 2001 United Nations projection, by the year 2050, the global population could very likely reach 9.3 billion. Will there be enough food, water, homes, jobs, and resources for all these people? It is difficult to say.

However, if one considers that 97 percent of this increase is expected to take place in poorer countries, it becomes clear that without adequate food, sanitary conditions, education, and economic opportunities, a rising population will be a major challenge to sustainability. Developing nations in Latin America, Africa, and parts of Asia are already struggling with poverty, hunger, disease, and lack of basic services such as education, health, and access to energy and fresh water. Imagine the pressure on the earth's already strained resources with another three billion people living on the planet. Consequences could include food shortages, health problems, and a damaged environment. As the British magazine the *Economist* asked prior to the 2002 Earth Summit in Johannesburg, "How many planets will we need if we continue to develop at the same rate?"

Interestingly, in the world's developed areas—North America, Australia, most of Europe, and parts of Asia such as Singapore and Japan—birth rates have actually been declining for some time now. This decrease, coupled with the successful introduction of family-planning methods in many developing countries where birth control was not traditionally practiced, will prevent the disastrous population explosion that scientists feared was certain to occur in the near future. In fact, current research shows that over the past forty years, the total global birth rate has actually decreased by half. Today, demographers (experts who study population trends) predict that after peaking around 2050, the world population will probably begin to fall, eventually settling at approximately eight billion people.

POVERTY

How is sustainable development a possibility on a planet with fewer well-off people and an increasing number of poor ones? Poverty is an extremely complicated issue that seems difficult to solve. While ideas on how to end poverty abound, putting the ideas into practice and seeing them actually improve people's lives has proven, at best, to be a very mixed experience.

Between 1950 and 1990, the world economy's annual output soared from $6.2 trillion to $31 trillion. Then in the ten years from 1990 to 2000 it quickly shot up to $42 trillion. So, if many more valuable goods and products are being made and so many riches are available, why is there so much poverty?

The problem is that a great deal of the wealth produced remains in the hands of a minority of the world's population, most of whom live in North America and western Europe. Since 1990, income of citizens of the world's forty wealthiest nations has grown by 3 percent every year. Meanwhile, between 1995 and 2005, people's incomes in over eighty other countries have declined. While there are some extremely wealthy people in Latin American and African countries, they often represent less than 5 percent of their country's population. Today,

With more than twenty million inhabitants, India's capital, Delhi, is the world's fifth-largest city. Despite the city's booming economy, millions continue to live in poverty. Above, people wait for food outside of a Muslim shrine. Worshippers whose prayers have been answered often give offerings of food to the hungry masses clustered around temples.

one billion people live on less than a dollar a day. Two billion more survive on less than two dollars a day.

Reducing poverty is one of the most difficult and urgent tasks facing world leaders today. Programs focused on improving health and education have produced some positive breakthroughs. Compared with thirty years ago, there are on average 50 percent fewer infant deaths, life expectancy has increased by almost ten years, the literacy rate is almost 80 percent, and there are 100 million fewer undernourished people

Education is one of the key issues in the global fight against poverty. Above, an instructor teaches health and nutrition to poor women and children in the city of Chennai, India. Formerly known as Madras, it is the automobile capital of India. Eighty percent of the country's vehicles are produced there, earning it the nickname the Detroit of South Asia.

around the globe. At the same time, however, between five and six million people in developing countries die each year as a result of air pollution and diseases caused by unclean water. Every year, over two million children under the age of five die from respiratory system infections. Sixty percent of these illnesses are caused by inadequate sanitation. Without money for cooking or heating fuel, poor people are forced to burn inexpensive, often poisonous materials—frequently in small, closed spaces. The results are filthy air, and land and water that become so polluted that they are unable to support the crops, animals, and fish that provide sustenance and economic livelihood.

HEALTH

In spite of medical progress, much of the world's population is increasingly faced with infectious diseases. Unsurprisingly, these diseases and who is affected

A child runs alongside a polluted drain in a slum on the banks of the Ozama River in Santo Domingo, Dominican Republic.

are directly related to environment. In developing countries with poor health conditions, there is little access to medical care, and medication is lacking or extremely expensive. As a result, millions are infected with and die from preventable (and often curable) diseases such as AIDS, malaria, and hepatitis. Over 90 percent of people with AIDS live in poor, developing nations. In many African countries in particular, between 20 and 40 percent of adults are infected with the virus.

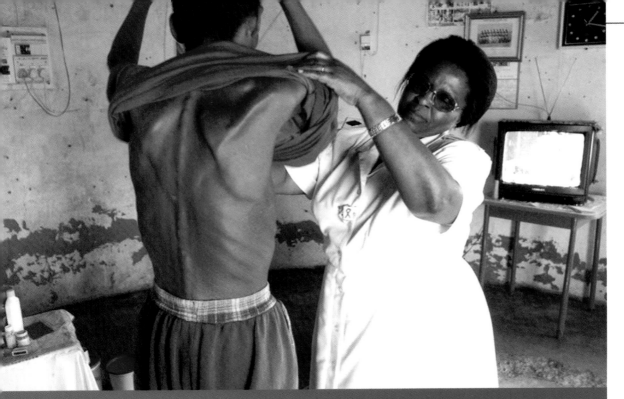

In Hlabisa, South Africa, Ellen Dube helps Obed Ndwandwe, who has AIDS, get undressed. The region around Hlabisa has South Africa's highest rate of HIV and AIDS. A report by the U.S. Agency for International Development estimates that by 2010, close to twenty-eight million African children will have lost at least one parent to AIDS.

While in 2000, the average life expectancy in developed countries was seventy-eight years, in poorer nations it was sixty-four.

Such diseases are preventable and now rarely kill inhabitants of developed nations. However, eating and driving more, exercising less, and stress contribute to "diseases of wealth" such as cancer, heart disease, and diabetes. Overeating and lack of physical activity, for example, increase the risk of heart disease. Currently, over 1.2 billion people worldwide are overweight. The United States' population, almost a third of whom are considered obese, is the most overweight in the world.

What do all of these diseases have in common? They are caused by a lack of sustainable development. Conditions like dirty water that breeds malaria-carrying mosquitoes in poor nations, and developed countries' dependence on automobiles that cause pollution and discourage exercise, increase the possibility of these illnesses. If such conditions are addressed, the population and environment would be better off.

CITIES

At the moment, close to half the people in the world live in cities. Cities offer many social, cultural, and economic

Fact for Thought

The United Nations estimates that for $75 billion a year, all major problems in the developing world could be solved, giving everyone clean drinking water, sanitation, basic health care, and education. In November of 2003, close to this amount ($70.6 billion) was set aside by the United States Congress to fund the American war in Iraq. As of September 30, 2005, $204.6 billion from U.S. taxpayers had been spent on the Iraq War.

A gigantic drainpipe runs through the center of Bandra *(above)*, in Mumbai, India. Each year, hundreds of thousands of migrants come to Mumbai looking for jobs. A vast majority of them end up living in slums or on the streets, joining the same fate as 60 percent of Mumbai's total population.

services and opportunities and can be wonderfully diverse places to live. However, as cities continue to grow rapidly, they often become overcrowded and polluted, and face rising crime levels.

In the developing world in particular, cities are growing at an astounding rate. Depleted resources and lack of basic services in rural areas cause poor people to move in the hopes of bettering their lives. However, without money, jobs, or often education, these migrants

Throwaway Culture

As countries around the world become increasingly industrialized, more products are made, purchased, and thrown on garbage heaps. It is not surprising that the United States, the wealthiest and most industrialized nation on Earth, is the world's biggest consumer. It is also the biggest producer of garbage. In the past forty years alone, the daily waste output of the average American has doubled from 2.2 to 4.4 pounds (1 to 2 kilograms).

While citizens of wealthy countries create up to 1,764 pounds (800 kg) of garbage every year, residents of poorer nations produce less than 441 pounds (200 kg). Around 95 percent of the garbage produced by developing countries consists of food and other natural waste that will decompose over time. The problem is that between 60 and 75 percent of developing nations' garbage is not collected or properly disposed of. In cities, this is a serious problem since most trash rots in streets and open spaces, polluting the environment and spreading infectious diseases.

Developed nations such as Canada and the United States have better waste management programs. They even recycle a significant amount of garbage (in the United States, for example, more than a third of all waste is recycled). However, much of the thrown-away waste consists of man-made, manu-factured materials ranging from plastics to high-tech electronic components from mechanical equipment and computers. Not only do these elements fail to decompose, but they contain toxic chemicals that are hazardous to the environment and to people's health.

find themselves living in shacks on city outskirts. Known as slums, these urban areas often have no plumbing, electricity, sewage systems, or running water. For example, in Addis Ababa, the capital of Ethiopia, less than 1 percent of homes are connected to a main water supply. In most major African cities, more than 50 percent of the population lives in slums. Frequently, frustrated and jobless inhabitants have no option but to turn to crime in order to survive.

Cities are currently not very sustainable. While they take up less than 2 percent of the earth's land surface, their inhabitants consume 75 percent of the planet's natural resources. Cities also create a great deal of pollution and waste, which contaminate surrounding land, water, and air. Today, over 1.5 billion people live in cities where air pollution—largely the result of automobile exhaust that emits poisonous nitrogen dioxide fumes—is above levels accepted by the World Health Organization (WHO). These cities in developed nations include New York, London, and Milan. In recent years, industrial pollution control has actually improved air quality in most North American and other industrialized countries' cities. In the rapidly expanding cities of Asia, Africa, and Latin America, however, conditions are getting much worse.

2

LAND

Birds hover around the Weltevreden landfill on the outskirts of Johannesburg, South Africa.

At the Rio Earth Summit in 1992, political and business leaders, scientists, environmentalists, and other participants agreed that human life depended upon the essential goods and services provided by the great variety of species and ecosystems found in nature. Agenda 21, the report that summed up the summit's debates and conclusions, warned that "the current decline in biodiversity is largely the result of human activity and represents a serious threat to human development."

This photograph shows burning of the Amazon rain forest in Brazil. The rain forest is being destroyed at a steady rate for farming, logging, mining, and the building of roads.

More than fifteen years later, it appears that this severe warning has been largely ignored. Every year, thirty-six million acres of forest are cut down or burned. According to the World Conservation Union, over 15,500 plant and animal species are listed as critically endangered, endangered, or vulnerable as of the end of 2004. This figure marks an increase of more than 3,000 from the previous year. And 25 percent of the earth's total land area has become desert.

Until recently, experts were stumped about how to save the earth from increasing damage. Protecting nature, and using and developing its resources for humans' growing needs, seemed like two contradictory goals. However, since the 2002 Johannesburg Summit, experts have begun to think that development without harming the environment is a very real possibility.

People are starting to view sustainability from a developmental view instead of an environmental view. Rather than saving the earth at the expense of development (or vice versa), environmental groups and industry and government leaders feel that they can bring together both goals. They believe the answer lies in considering, first and foremost, how to improve people's lives. Since human lives will only get better if they have access to a well-maintained, healthy, and diverse environment, the solution is to come up with plans and projects by which people can better their living and economic situations by preserving and even improving their natural surroundings. More and more, people are discovering that this occurs when plans are carried out on a local level where residents have a stake in their success. Instead of following a one-size-fits-all global strategy, people are taking into account the ecosystems and different needs of their own specific regions, and finding that real, workable results can take place.

BIODIVERSITY

Biodiversity refers to the variety of life—plants, animals, and micro-organisms as well as their genes—in a given ecosystem. The earth is presently experiencing the largest extinction of plant and animal species since dinosaurs disappeared over sixty-five million years ago. Humans are to blame for most of this extinction. Furthermore, scientists fear that if we don't change our behavior, as

This illustration shows the diversity of animals—from raccoons and screech owls to gray tree frogs and wood-boring beetle grubs—that contribute to the ecosystem of a forest in the American Midwest. When a tree dies, it continues to provide homes to many animals. Fungi and bacteria help decompose the tree, allowing nutrients to return to the soil where they act like fertilizer to promote the growth of new trees.

many as half of all known species on the planet could disappear by the end of the twenty-first century.

Aside from making the earth an uglier place, destroying other species means that we are destroying ourselves. Even altering small ecosystems can have disastrous effects. Plants and animals provide humans with essential food and medicines that cannot be manufactured. And, as we have become more globalized, people and goods are traveling with increasing ease and frequency from one country to another. Many plants, animals, insects, and microbes (such as germs and viruses) have migrated with this movement from one ecosystem to another. Such "invasions" can have damaging effects on entire ecosystems, such as forests, fields, and swamps. They can also harm individual organisms, from wild plants and animals to crops, farm animals, and human beings. Diseases and even death can result since neither ecosystems nor their inhabitants are naturally equipped to defend themselves from foreign species.

Bird flu vaccine is injected into a chicken in Shanghai, China. Chinese health inspectors now routinely visit homes, farms, and bird preserves to ensure that adequate measures are being followed to prevent the spread of this deadly strain of flu that has recently infected humans.

FROM FIELDS TO FORESTS

Human activities have been responsible for the disappearance, at a record rate, of natural wilderness spaces. Clearing of fields and forests for farms or livestock grazing has led to the expansion of deserts. Desertification is

In Queensland, Australia, large-scale cutting down of trees and cattle grazing has caused once fertile soil to be eroded by rain and winds.

often the result of lack of water and overuse of land through intensive farming. Meanwhile, half of the earth's original forests no longer exist. Most of this loss took place in the twentieth century with the growth of large-scale cultivation and cutting down of trees for wood and paper.

Aside from destroying ancient ecosystems, many of which will never return, the loss of forests has been directly linked to an increase in natural disasters. Without tree roots to anchor it, soil erodes and is easily washed away. Such erosion can result in catastrophic landslides and flooding. In part, the devastating floods that struck the U.S. Gulf Coast in the September 2005 wake of Hurricane Katrina were the result of years of soil erosion caused by the clearing of wilderness for urban development.

Although many wilderness areas have been destroyed, there is hope for the future. A number of countries, including Canada and the United States, have passed strict reforestation laws. In California, for example,

Landfills

A landfill is an enormous garbage heap. In developed countries, landfills are often well-designed, closed-off, monitored spaces. Waste is dumped with minimal exposure to humans and the environment. In poorer nations, landfills tend to be fully exposed mountains of garbage located close to the poorest neighborhoods or city suburbs. Many people, particularly children, survive by picking through the harmful, often poisonous trash and selling scraps like aluminum cans and computer parts.

The Al-Tagi landfill, on the outskirts of Iraq's capital, Baghdad, stretches as far as the eye can see.

Besides destroying plants and animals, these concentrations of waste—which contain everything from detergents, bleaches, and rusty metals to dangerous chemicals—seep into the earth, damaging soil and poisoning water supplies. The effects of living near landfills can range from infections and respiratory diseases to birth defects in children. The presence of fuels and other chemicals also make landfills a fire hazard. When fires break out, they release toxins, creating polluted air that is hazardous to breathe. Such fires are believed to be a major source of dioxins. Dioxins are toxic natural substances produced when man-made materials such as garbage are burned. They are present in many industrial products ranging from cigarettes to plastics to bleaches. Humans and wildlife can't avoid breathing in some small amount of dioxins, but in large quantities, over time, they can be deadly.

seven trees are planted for every tree that is harvested. Meanwhile, the coffee company Starbucks, working with the Washington, D.C.-based Center for Environmental Leadership in Business, has adopted a policy that rewards coffee planters around the world whose growing methods do the least harm to the environment. Such policies work because they make both business and environmental sense while giving workers incentive to take care of the environment as part of their jobs.

FOOD

The world produces more than enough food for the entire global population. Since the early 1960s, production of meat and fish has almost quadrupled, while that of grains and cereals has doubled. High-yielding seeds, fertilizers, pesticides, and high-tech equipment have resulted in larger agricultural harvests than ever before. If there is such an abundance of food, however, why is it that more than 800 million people (13 percent of the world's population) go hungry?

With developing countries in the Southern Hemisphere in urgent need of money, their governments and businesses often depend upon and encourage "industrial agriculture." This involves the cultivation of a few selected crops that can be easily produced, sold, and shipped to industrial nations in the Northern

In Zimbabwe, a couple plant and harvest bananas, pineapples, gooseberries, coffee, and maize (a type of corn) on less than 2.5 acres (1 hectare) of land. Rather than being used to feed themselves, the crops will be sold as cash crops and exported to other countries.

Hemisphere (who purchase them at inexpensive prices). Such "cash crops" can be easily exported, but they do not solve hunger problems in their countries of origin.

In fact, while items such as corn and soy are being produced globally, more families in developing countries who grow and harvest these crops are going hungry. The emphasis on profitable cash crops means that instead of locally cultivating a wide variety of food that can meet the needs of their communities and livestock, many people must rely on food that is imported from other places. Taxes and the costs of transportation by ship, plane, or truck over vast distances drive up the prices of these imported foods, making them unaffordable to most.

It is a tremendous irony that food flows from areas of hunger and poverty to regions of overabundance and that the majority of the world's hungriest people are farm workers. Meanwhile, the creation of large-scale agricultural or livestock farms destroys entire ecosystems. Many fertilizers and pesticides contain chemicals that strip fertile soil of its natural nutrients. As a result, people abandon barren land and begin to clear forests and other wilderness territories, often resorting to inexpensive, but potentially destructive "slash and burn" methods. With depleted natural resources and damaged, unfertile soil, how can we expect to feed future generations?

Intensive vs. Organic Farming

Around the world, both small, individual farmers and large, agricultural businesses are preparing to meet the food demands of a growing population. However, how can they do this without harming the environment they depend upon to provide them with their food?

Organic farmers use only natural methods. They believe in raising fruits, vegetable, grains, and animals without relying upon chemical pesticides and fertilizers. Chemicals can make crops and soil more resistant to severe weather and diseases. Adding drugs to animals' diets can make them fatter and therefore increase meat production. However, organic farmers disagree with such methods, claiming that these practices harm the environment and are dangerous to human health.

Intensive farmers, on the other hand, believe that such technology has allowed great quantities of food to be produced in an efficient manner. Farmers gain economic benefits, and the rest of the world has access to more food at a cheaper price. Some scientists suggest that if all chemical fertilizers were removed overnight, the world's grain output would decrease by half.

Increasingly, experts believe that the most sustainable solution is a mixture of both organic and intensive methods. For example, if farmers had better knowledge about how to capture the most light and water, prevent weeds, and minimize insect attacks, they could rely less on harmful chemicals and minimize soil damage. Computers and high-tech measuring equipment could help farmers to discover exactly what nutrients are lacking in the soil. Then, when they do use fertilizer, they wouldn't use too much or too little, but just enough to replenish what was lost.

3

WATER AND AIR

A beach in Mumbai, India, is littered with garbage. Fishermen complain that water pollution has greatly diminished the number of fish they catch, even in deep waters.

If 70 percent of the earth consists of water, how is it that more than one billion people are without access to this most essential life-maintaining liquid? The problem is that only 2.5 percent of the planet's water is fresh and just a small percentage of it is directly available to humans. (In fact, around 70 percent of the world's freshwater is found in the frozen ice of the Antarctic polar cap.) As pollution and drought continue to contaminate and diminish already insufficient quantities of water, what can be done to safeguard increasingly precious supplies for future generations?

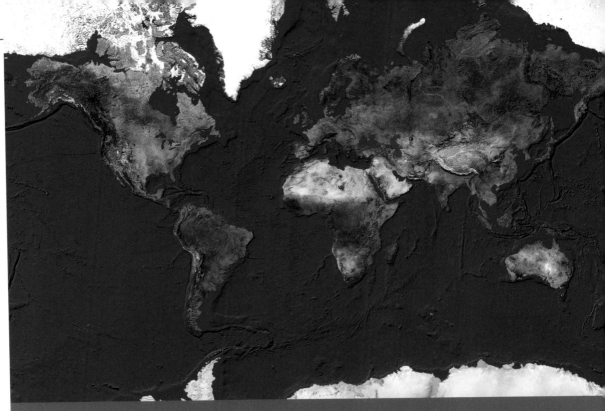

This true-color satellite map of the world shows the earth's land cover and oceans. It gives an idea of how the planet would look to an astronaut in space: blue water, green vegetation, brown areas of dry desert, and white snow and ice.

FRESHWATER

On average, a person needs around fifty quarts (forty-seven liters) of water a day for basic needs such as drinking, washing, and cooking. However, the United Nations estimates that by 2025, two-thirds of the earth's population may be dealing with severe water shortages. The destruction of delicate freshwater ecosystems is just as serious as the lack of access to freshwater. In the last hundred years, lake and river pollution, large-scale diversion of water for dams, and draining of wetlands

In Beijing, China's capital and second-largest city (with a population of 15 million people), a man shovels garbage from a water canal. A negative side effect of China's economic boom is a rise in water pollution that could leave rapidly expanding cities with a lack of clean drinking water. Already, over 100 of the country's 660 cities face water shortages.

for urban and agricultural development have killed off and endangered many freshwater species and their habitats. Currently, more than 20 percent of all aquatic life on the planet faces possible extinction. In North America, close to 40 percent of species are at risk.

How can this alarming trend be reversed at the same time that so many people are still without water? Experts believe that the solution lies less in reducing our intake of water than in using it more intelligently. Two-thirds of water used is for agriculture. More efficient irrigation techniques such as using continuous drips of water instead of wasteful sprinklers or hoses, for example, would use much less water. So would planting crops engineered and bred by biologists to require less water and resist droughts. Such crops are already being developed in various African countries. One successful example has been the bambara groundnut, a type of chickpea that is native to the continent. Aside from being highly nutritious

In furrow irrigation *(above)*, a series of small channels are dug into the soil to transport water. This method uses less water, costs less, and results in larger harvests.

and rich in protein (on a continent where diets are often lacking in meat and fish), the bambara groundnut can thrive in arid desert areas where most other crops cannot.

Adopting these solutions for agriculture would make more water available for humans. Currently, 2.4 billion people lack water for basic sanitary needs such as washing. The absence of sewage systems exposes many people to dangerous germs, viruses, and diseases. In developing nations, between 90 and 95 percent of sewage and 70 percent of industrial waste is dumped into water supplies without being treated. To improve this situation, the United Nations, along with many governments and nongovernmental organizations (NGOs), has pledged to provide water services and hygiene training to all countries without them by 2015. This program is known as WASH (Water, Sanitation and Hygiene for All), and is organized by the Water Supply and Sanitation Collaborative Council (WSSCC).

OCEANS

Oceans cover close to three-quarters of the planet. Humans tend to think of these immense and deep bodies of water as infinite in the resources (such as fish) they contain and the pollution (ranging from sewage to oil spills) they can absorb. Over the last ten years, however, research has shown that oceans are reaching their limits in terms of what they can give and take.

Throughout the world, and particularly in poorer nations, humans have always depended on the sea for their food and livelihood. But what happens when pollution, combined with overexploitation, reduces populations of fish and other marine life to dangerously low levels? At the moment, close to 70 percent of the most commercialized fish species are being overfished. Sometimes this fishing is done using illegal and uncontrolled methods that severely damage marine life.

Dynamiting or blast fishing, for example, is an illegal method used to kill fish. Dynamite or homemade bombs are thrown into the sea. The shock of the explosion kills fish (and many other forms of sea life) and leaves them floating on the water's surface where they can be easily collected. Overfishing not only means less food for humans, but it also results in ocean ecosystems where some species are left without sustenance

Oil spills are common in the Niger Delta, located along Nigeria's coast. When cleanups happen, they are often poorly done. Here, a Nigerian man tries to clean up an oil spill with a bowl and sticks.

while others multiply beyond control. Additional problems are created by the human and industrial wastes that enter the sea. Whether accidental, such as oil spills, or deliberate, such as garbage, pollution does enormous harm to oceans and coastal areas as well as to the plants and animals that live in or around them.

Rising Seas

Scientists say that the world's ocean levels are increasing at an alarming rate. Currently, the seas are rising at around 0.08 inches (2 millimeters) a year, which is faster than at any time over the last 5,000 years. Of even greater concern is the prediction from multiple sources, including the World Wildlife Fund (WWF) and the National Wetlands Research Center (NWRC), that over the next 100 years, this rate will likely increase to 0.4 inches (5 mm) a year. According to the Intergovern-mental Panel on Climate Change (IPCC), whose estimates are based on highly sensitive ocean sensors and precise satellite measurements, by 2100 world sea levels are likely to have risen overall by 10 to 30 inches (25 to 76 centimeters). Such an increase could have a devastating effect on coastal cities and farmland around the world, causing flooding, deaths, and destruction of ecosystems and property. Already, entire islands, like Tuvalu in the South Pacific Ocean and the Maldives in the Indian Ocean, are threatened with being submerged.

Seas are rising because local climate warming trends and human actions have caused the planet to heat up. As temperatures rise, ancient ice sheets called glaciers in the Alps, Andes, and Rockies, and Antarctic and Arctic polar ice sheets are melting like never before. This melting adds considerably to the planet's volume of seawater. As polar ice caps diminish, seawater also becomes warmer. Warmer water not only expands to take up more volume, but it can also damage fragile marine ecosystems.

The Great Barrier Reef off the east coast of Australia is the world's largest coral reef. More than 1,243 miles (2,000 kilometers) long, it is home to over 1,500 types of fish. Scientists predict that temperatures along the reef will rise by up to six degrees Fahrenheit (fourteen degrees Celsius) by the end of 2100. A change of even one degree in sea temperature can kill coral. The result is that by 2050 less than 5 percent of the reef coral will be alive. Not only does this mean the disappearance of the beautifully colored fish that live in these waters, but it means the loss of a valuable food source and jobs as well as close to $1 billion a year in revenues from tourism and fishing.

This aerial photograph shows two of the many reefs that make up Australia's Great Barrier Reef. With its unique marine ecosystem threatened, in 2003 it became the world's most protected reef.

AIR

The earth's land and water are not the only natural regions threatened by human activity. Air has also suffered

Through Beijing's smog and haze, the Forbidden City, the ancient palace of China's emperors, is barely visible. China's air pollution problem is worsened by the burning of coal for fuel and increased automobile traffic. As the nation's middle class has expanded, more people have been buying cars, making China the world's fastest-growing automobile market.

damage. Many of the world's cities produce unacceptable levels of air pollution. Caused by industrial waste and automobile exhaust fumes, this dirty air creates serious health problems for many people. In some parts of southern Asia, for example, heavy air pollution has created a permanent haze known as the Asian brown cloud. Two miles (3.2 km) thick, it is thought to cause hundreds of thousands of deaths from respiratory diseases each year. Waste gases have also harmed the

Ozone Hole

The ozone layer is a region in the atmosphere about 6 to 31 miles (9.7 to 50 km) from Earth's surface where there is a concentration of the ozone (O_3) molecule. It forms a natural shield that protects Earth from the sun's harmful ultraviolet (UV) rays, which can cause severe sunburn and skin cancer. Human activity, however, has been largely responsible for destroying the ozone layer. One of the main culprits is human-made chlorofluorocarbons (CFCs), which are used and released into the air by cars, cleaners, and aerosols. As a result, increasingly large holes are appearing in the ozone layer, particularly in the Southern Hemisphere.

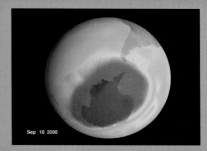

Sep 10 2000

This satellite image shows one of the largest ozone "holes," recorded in 2000.

earth's atmosphere. These gases, produced by humans, are particularly damaging. Burning of fossil fuels such as coal, oil, and wood cause carbon dioxide and other greenhouse gases to be released into the atmosphere.

All animals, including human beings, produce carbon dioxide. After breathing in oxygen, they exhale it into the air. In the atmosphere, carbon dioxide, along with ozone, functions like a sponge to soak up heat from the earth's surface. This natural "greenhouse" effect helps make the earth warm enough to sustain life. However, the burning of fossil fuels and other gases produces

Incineration

Incinerating, or burning, waste is a common way of dealing with garbage. Incineration has many advantages. It can reduce the weight of a mountain of garbage by 75 percent and cut its volume by up to 90 percent. If done properly in a specially equipped plant, the heat given off by incineration can be used as an energy source.

Incineration also has its downsides. Burning garbage releases greenhouse gases into the atmosphere. Not only does this cause air pollution, but it also contributes to global warming. Furthermore, incineration releases harmful poisonous chemicals, gases, dirt, and dust into the air. High-tech incineration systems can prevent many of these polluting substances from contaminating the air by a process similar to a cleansing filter. However, the systems are expensive and many industries are unwilling or unable to spend the money required. In addition, governments do not always monitor waste incineration as they should.

even more carbon dioxide. Scientists believe that this is causing the earth's climate to warm at a faster rate than ever before recorded. This phenomenon, called global warming, is thought to be the cause of many recent changes on the earth, from rising temperatures and sea levels to the melting of glaciers and polar caps. It is also thought to be responsible for an increase in severe weather events such as droughts, floods, tidal waves, and hurricanes.

4   ENERGY

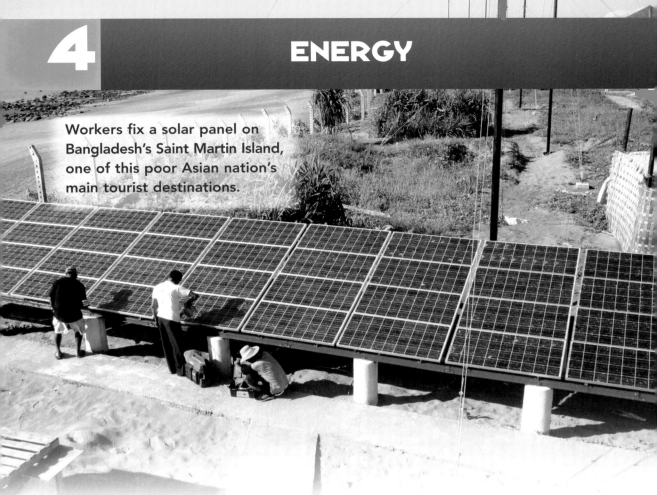

Workers fix a solar panel on Bangladesh's Saint Martin Island, one of this poor Asian nation's main tourist destinations.

As early as 5,000 to 6,000 years ago, ancient civilizations had discovered and were using fossil fuels, primarily as sources of light and heat. Today, fossil fuels provide much of our energy. Burning fossil fuels such as coal, gas, and oil creates the energy that allows us to heat our homes; drive cars, buses, and airplanes; and power the machinery that runs our industrial society. Aside from their negative impact on the environment, fossil fuels are soon going to run out. Based on current consumption rates, coal supplies could last for another 200 years or so, but oil and natural gas

43

A miner stands outside the Karkar coal mine in Afghanistan. The nation still relies heavily on coal for energy. The miners who work here earn less than four dollars a day.

will likely disappear worldwide before the end of the twenty-first century.

FOSSIL FUELS

Coal, oil, and natural gas are called fossil fuels because, for the most part, they were formed approximately 300 million years ago. This age, which preceded the arrival of dinosaurs, is known as the Carboniferous period. "Carboniferous" refers to the element carbon, which is present in all fossil fuels. During the Carboniferous period, the earth was covered with huge trees and leafy plants. When they died, they sank to the bottoms of swamps and oceans and formed layers of a sponge-like substance called peat. Over the centuries, the peat was covered with sand and other minerals, which formed rocks. As these rocks piled up, they pressed down heavily on the peat, causing the water to be squeezed out of it. Over millions of years, this new substance deep beneath the rock was slowly transformed. Depending on the

Fact for Thought

Americans, in particular, count on natural oil, also known as petroleum, above all other fossil fuels. Petroleum is used to make gasoline, diesel oil, jet fuel, home heating oil, and the oil that is burned in power plants to make electricity. Furthermore, when refined or purified, petroleum is an essential ingredient in an astounding array of products ranging from clothing and fertilizers to all kinds of plastics. Did you know that the plastic pen you write with and the comb you brush your hair with are made from oil?

types of organic material it contained, it became a solid (coal), liquid (oil), or gas (natural gas).

Currently, the United States uses more than a quarter of the world's energy (over 80 percent of which is from fossil fuels), and this number is only expected to rise. Over the last fifty years alone, Americans' energy consumption has more than quadrupled. Today, the United States is the world's largest producer, consumer, and importer of energy.

The big problem is that fossil fuels take millions of years to make. They are neither renewable nor recyclable. Even if we reduce our consumption, we are still due to run out of them as early as the next century. And this is without considering the fact that more than two billion people around the world are without electricity. As these people gradually gain access to energy, fossil fuels will disappear at an even more alarming rate. And as these fuels become more rare, they will become more expensive. Already around the world, higher costs of oil have sent prices of heating, car gasoline, and jet fuel soaring. In fact, oil is often referred to as "black gold."

ALTERNATIVE ENERGY SOURCES

Many people, particularly North Americans, waste energy leaving on their house lights and heat, for example, and driving gas-guzzling SUVs. Conservation of fossil fuels is not enough, however. Alternative sources of energy need to be found that are renewable, less expensive, available to all, and don't harm the environment.

Some such sources actually already exist and are being used in various places around the world, including—on a small scale—in North America. Governments are the biggest obstacles to their widespread acceptance. Laws must be passed that will persuade individuals and businesses to invest in and adopt these sources in manners that are affordable and sustainable while discouraging use of oil and other fossil fuels. In India, for example, there has been an increase in energy that comes from wind power. This is because the Indian government made it easier for businesses to acquire technology and equipment for converting wind to energy. It then required state power companies to buy the electricity produced by these wind systems. Other countries are experimenting with alternate technologies. The key to success will be finding the right energy source for specific users. For example, ocean power is a promising solution for island populations, while people living in deserts can readily adopt solar power.

ALTERNATIVE ENERGY SOLUTIONS

Solar Energy

If you've used a pocket calculator, you may have seen solar power at work on a small scale. Materials called semiconductors can transmit electric currents when they are arranged in a series and sunlight shines on them. If arranged in large panels, for example, and exposed to the sun, they can receive enough light to provide electricity to an entire household or building. Although demand for solar energy has grown about 25 percent a year over the past fifteen years, solar energy still accounts for less than 0.01 percent of total global energy production.

Wind Energy

Humans have used wind power for centuries. In Europe, in particular, windmills were used to pump water and grind grain. Today, modern windmills known as wind turbines use giant propellers to harness the wind's energy. Wind blowing through the turbines' enormous blades,

India is among the top five world leaders in the production and usage of wind power. Germany, Spain, the United States, and Denmark are the others.

some of which span more than 100 feet (30 meters) in length, drives a generator that transforms the mechanical energy into electrical energy. Although areas with numerous turbines, called wind farms, have been increasing in number by around 40 percent a year since 1995, they still only produce around 0.5 percent of the world's energy.

Nuclear Energy

Uranium is a natural chemical element found in low levels in most rocks, soil, and water. Large amounts of uranium come from Canada and Australia in particular. It is used to create nuclear energy because it is a highly radioactive element (it releases toxic rays into the atmosphere around it). Nuclear energy is created by bombarding an atom (a tiny particle of matter) of uranium with a tinier subatomic particle such as a proton or neutron. This causes the atom to split and release a large amount of energy in the form of heat. It also releases other neutrons, which hit other

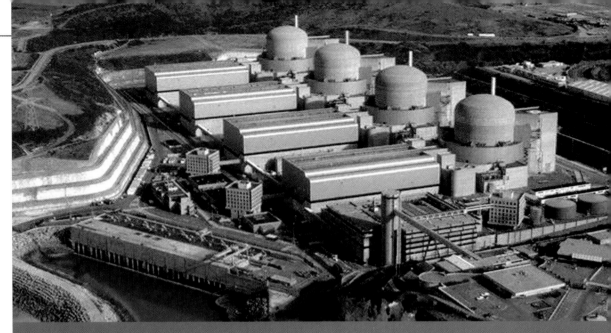

The Paluel nuclear power plant, above, is located at Veulettes on France's Normandy coast. France has been very active in developing nuclear technology. Seventy-five percent of its electricity comes from nuclear power. Another 15 percent is provided by hydro energy.

atoms, causing them to explode in a chain reaction. All of this activity takes place in a sealed-off plant known as a nuclear reactor, where atoms' reactions can be controlled. The intense heat the atoms release generates electricity.

Currently, nuclear power provides around 17 percent of the planet's electricity. Nuclear plants produce 75 percent of electricity in France, 25 percent in Great Britain, 8 percent in the United States, and 6 percent in Canada.

Hydro Energy

Hydropower involves using large amounts of flowing water to produce energy. Water from a dam runs downhill through a pipe. As the water flows, it turns a

Water flows through the open gates of the main dam of the Three Gorges project in Yichang, China. It is the world's biggest hydroelectric project to date.

giant turbine. The force and quantity of the water drives a huge electric generator, which transforms the mechanical energy from the turbine into electric energy. The water then can be pumped back up and reused. Twenty percent of the world relies on hydropower for its electricity. Despite the fact that it is 40 percent cheaper than fossil fuels, less than 5 percent of the United States' energy is generated from hydropower. Hydropower supplies 99 percent of Norway's energy needs, and 24 percent of Canada's.

Micro-hydroelectric plants in developing nations such as Sri Lanka and Kenya have made it possible for many communities without energy to have electricity. Without building vast dams and disturbing the surrounding environment, they divert water from nearby streams and rivers. A small community power plant can produce enough electricity for up to 500 homes and businesses. In these countries, some plants are built by villagers themselves, all of whom own shares in the company that sells the energy.

Hydrogen Energy

Pure hydrogen is a gas. In nature, however, hydrogen is often found combined with oxygen in water, coal, or oil. Initially, when hydrogen and oxygen combine, energy is released. Under controlled circumstances, this energy can be made to flow into a circuit that creates an electrical current. Non-polluting and efficient, hydrogen energy is viewed by specialists as one of the most promising alternative energy sources of the future. The small island nation of Iceland is already developing plans to become the world's first hydrogen economy.

Ocean Energy

The ocean offers many opportunities for energy production. Since oceans cover more than 70 percent of the earth's surface, these vast bodies of water are the world's largest collectors of solar energy. In theory, if less than 0.1 percent of this energy could be converted into electricity, it would supply twenty times the amount of energy consumed daily in the United States. Meanwhile, the movement of ocean waves and tides creates mechanical energy that can be converted into electricity. Since 2000, the world's first commercial wave power station in Scotland has been providing electricity to over 400 homes on the island of Islay.

Advantages and Disadvantages of Leading Alternative Energy Sources

ENERGY SOURCE	ADVANTAGES	DISADVANTAGES
Solar	• free • renewable • silent • non-polluting • solar panels can be integrated into the landscape • useful in isolated regions	• not necessarily the best option for cloudy regions and crowded cities • expensive to make solar panels (although the price has dropped as mass production has increased) • toxic chemicals are used to produce semiconductors
Wind	• safe • free • non-polluting • renewable	• wind isn't reliable or constant (can blow hard or not at all) • wind turbines can be noisy
Nuclear	• produces large quantities of energy without releasing green-house gases • not dependent on the weather	• fuel left over from nuclear power plants stays toxic for centuries and is difficult to store safely • the uranium used is a limited natural resource
Hydro	• non-polluting • renewable	• only suitable in places with a great deal of water (rain, rivers, lakes) • building dams means changing an ecosystem (flooding farmland, cutting down forests, and moving people and animals) • burst dams can cause flooding

ENERGY SOURCE	ADVANTAGES	DISADVANTAGES
Hydrogen	• since hydrogen occurs naturally in water, supplies are vast • silent • non-polluting	• difficult to isolate hydrogen (must use electricity to split water molecules, separating them into oxygen and hydrogen—an expensive process known as electrolysis) • bulky to transport • in its pure gas form, hydrogen is very flammable (easily catches fire) and thus potentially dangerous
Ocean	• free • silent • renewable	• only efficient for coastal areas
Geothermal	• free • silent • renewable	• most efficient in regions where geothermal activity (underwater hot springs and water jets, vapor, and steam, all heated by the earth's volcanic core) takes place close to the earth's surface
Bio	• very sustainable, since it recycles waste that would otherwise pollute • inexpensive • if done correctly, bioenergy pollutes much less than burning fossil fuels	• if burning of materials is not done correctly, it can be toxic, polluting air and resulting in fatal diseases

Geothermal Energy

This Scottish wave power generator was made from lightweight steel and designed to be used close to the ocean shore.

Geothermal energy comes from the heat beneath the earth's surface in its core. On volcanic Iceland, for example, most buildings are heated using geothermal energy. Underground hot water or steam is pumped to the surface. Under pressure, it can be made to turn turbines, creating electrical energy.

Bioenergy

Bioenergy is made from burning biological matter such as wood or plants. In many developing countries, simple forms of bioenergy—burning wood or animal dung to cook over or heat homes—are common. However, other nations use bioenergy as an inexpensive alternative to fossil fuels that also works to reduce waste. For instance, in Brazil, sugarcane is fermented and made into a type of alcohol called ethanol that is used as fuel for cars. Around 50 percent of Brazilians rely on ethanol, which is less expensive than gas and reduces carbon dioxide emissions by half.

HOPE FOR THE FUTURE

Now, in the early part of the twenty-first century, our planet's situation often seems bleak. In the media, we hear that global warming is causing catastrophes such as Hurricane Katrina, record melting of the Arctic ice cap, or all-time high levels of skin cancer due to holes in the atmosphere's ozone layer. Sometimes, so many disasters seem overwhelming.

Ultimately, the key to solving all of these problems doesn't require tremendous amounts of money or sweeping reforms, but human intelligence, adaptability, innovation, and cooperation. In terms of future energy sources, for example, we are starting to make progress. Solar- and wind-generated energy today costs a tenth of what it did ten years ago. Increasingly, governments are funding research and supporting reforms, private companies are developing new products and technologies, and a more aware and educated population is making changes in homes and communities. All of these forces coming together will improve lives without harming the planet and will continue to make sustainable development not just a dream but a reality.

GLOSSARY

AIDS (acquired immunodeficiency syndrome) A serious, chronic, and sometimes deadly disease transmitted when the HIV virus enters the human bloodstream and weakens the body's immune system.

atom A tiny basic particle of any type of matter.

biodiversity The different plants, animals, micro-organisms, and their genes that make up the earth's many regions, or ecosystems.

chlorofluorocarbons (CFCs) Chemical substances commonly used in refrigerators, air conditioners, fire extinguishers, and cleaning fluids that are highly toxic and harmful to the environment.

demographer A scientist who studies growth and changes in populations.

desertification Transformation of habitable land into desert, usually caused by climate change or destructive treatment of the soil.

dioxin A type of toxic natural material that is produced as a by-product of burning man-made materials such as garbage that contain chlorine.

ecosystem A system made up of the interaction between a group of living organisms and their natural environment.

erosion A process by which the earth's surface is worn away by the action of water and wind.

generator A machine that converts mechanical energy into electrical energy.

glacier An enormous sheet of moving ice.

global warming An increase in the temperature of the earth's atmosphere that causes the climate to change.

greenhouse effect Warming of the earth that results from increased greenhouse gases such as carbon dioxide absorbing the sun's heat and trapping it into the atmosphere.

neutron An essential part of an atom that possesses a neutral (i.e. no) electronic charge.

ozone layer A region in the atmosphere composed of ozone molecules, which forms a natural shield that protects the earth from the harmful effects of the sun's ultraviolet (UV) rays.

proton An essential part of an atom that possesses a positive electronic charge.

radioactivity The ability of some elements, such as uranium, to emit energy particles when their atoms break apart.

reforestation The replanting of a forest after trees have been burned or cut down.

semiconductor A substance that allows electrical currents to flow through it under certain circumstances.

slash-and-burn agriculture The practice of cutting down forests or fields, burning the cut and dried vegetation, and then planting crops in the ashes.

For more information

Energy Council of Canada
350 Sparks Street, Suite 608
Ottawa, ON K1R 7S8
Canada
(613) 232-8239
Web site: http://www.energy.ca/users/folder.asp

Environment Canada
70 Crémazie Street
Gatineau, QU K1A 0H3
Canada
(800) 668-6767 or (819) 997-2800
Web site: http://www.ec.gc.ca/environment_e.html

Intergovernmental Panel on Climate Control
IPCC Secretariat
c/o World Meteorological Organization
7bis Avenue de la Paix
C.P. 2300, CH-1211
Geneva, Switzerland
Web site: http://www.ipcc.ch

United Nations Division for Sustainable Development
Department of Economic and Social Affairs
Two United Nations Plaza, Room DC2-2220
New York, NY 10017

(212) 963-8102
Web site: http://www.un.org/esa/sustdev

United States Department of Energy
Energy Efficiency and Renewable Energy
Mail Stop EE-1
Washington, DC 20585
(202) 586-9220
Web site: http://www.eere.energy.gov

United States Environmental Protection Agency (EPA)
1200 Pennsylvania Avenue NW
Washington, DC 20460
(202) 272-0167
Web site: http://www.epa.gov

WEB SITES

Due to the changing nature of Internet links, the Rosen
Publishing Group, Inc., has developed an online list of
Web sites related to the subject of this book. This site is
updated regularly. Please use this link to access the list:

http://www.rosenlinks.com/eet/thrs

FOR FURTHER READING

Arthus-Bertrand. Yann. *The Future of the Earth: An Introduction to Sustainable Development for Young Readers*. New York, NY: Harry N. Abrams, 2004.

Bowdon, Rob. *Energy* (Sustainable World). Detroit, MI: KidHaven Press, 2004.

Craig, Claire, and Sharon Dalgeish, et al. *The Edge of Extinction*. New York, NY: Chelsea House, 2004.

Gareth, Carol Ballard. *The Search for Better Conservation*. Milwaukee, WI: Gareth Stevens, 2005.

Hirschmann, Kris. *Pollution* (Our Environment). Detroit, MI: KidHaven Press, 2004.

Mongillo, John, and Peter Mongillo. *Teen Guides to Environmental Sciences*. Five Volumes (Earth Systems and Ecology, Resources and Energy, People and Their Environments, Human Impact on the Environment, and Creating a Sustainable Society). Westport, CT: Greenwood Press, 2004.

Petersen, Christine. *Alternative Energy*. New York, NY: Scholastic, 2004.

BIBLIOGRAPHY

BBC.com. "Disposable Planet?" Retrieved September 2005 (http://news.bbc.co.uk/hi/english/static/in_depth/world/2002/disposable_planet/default.stm).

Energy Council of Canada. "Energy Information." Retrieved September 2005 (http://www.energy.ca/users/folder.asp?FolderID=2480).

Forum for the Future. Retrieved September 2005 (http://www.forumforthefuture.org.uk).

GreenFacts.org. "Scientific Facts on Ecosystem Change." Retrieved September 2005 (http://www.greenfacts.org/ecosystems).

Millennium Ecosystem Assessment. Retrieved September 2005 (http://www.millenniumassessment.org/en/index.aspx).

PBS.org. "NOW with Bill Moyers: The Earth Debate." Retrieved September 2005 (http://www.pbs.org/now/science/unsummit.html).

PBS.org. "Think Tank with Ben Wattenberg. Transcript for Sustainable Development." PBS.com. Retrieved September 2005 (http://www.pbs.org/thinktank/transcript1010.html).

Shah, Anup. "Sustainable Development." Global Issues.org. Retrieved September 2005 (http://www.globalissues.org/TradeRelated/Development.asp).

Time.com. "The Green Century." Retrieved September 2005 (http://www.time.com/time/2002/greencentury/index.html).

United Nations Division on Sustainable Development—Commission on Sustainable Development (CSD). Retrieved September 2005 (http://www.un.org/esa/sustdev/).

United States Department of Energy: Energy Efficiency and Renewable Energy. Retrieved September 2005 (http://www.eere.energy.gov/).

Worldwatch Institute. Retrieved September 2005 (http://www.worldwatch.org/).

INDEX

A

Agenda 21, 7, 21
AIDS, 15

B

biodiversity, 21, 23–25

C

cities, 17–20

D

desertification, 22, 25–26
dioxins, 27
disease, 11, 15–17, 27, 35, 40

E

Earth Summits, 6–8, 11, 21, 22
endangered/extinct plants/animals, 22, 23–24

energy sources
    biological matter, 53, 54
    fossil fuels, 41, 43–46, 50
    geothermal, 53, 54
    hydrogen, 51, 53
    nuclear, 48–49, 52
    solar, 47, 52, 55
    water/ocean, 47, 49–51, 52, 53
    wind, 46, 47–48, 52, 55

F

farming
    cash crops, 28–29
    fertilizers, 30, 31
    intensive vs. organic, 30–31
    irrigation techniques, 34–35
fishing, 5, 36–37, 39
forests, destruction of, 22, 25, 26, 30
freshwater, 11, 32, 33–36

G

garbage, 19, 27, 37, 42
global warming, 42, 55
Great Barrier Reef, 39
greenhouse effect, 41

I

incineration, 42
industrial agriculture, 28–29
infectious diseases, 15–16

L

landfills, 27

M

Millennium Ecosystem Assessment,
    8–9

O

ozone layer, 41, 55

P

petroleum, 45
pollution
    air, 5, 14, 15, 20, 39–42
    freshwater, 33–34
    of oceans, 36–39
population growth, 5, 10–12
    birth rates, 11
    effects on cities, 17–20
    and poor health conditions,
        15–17
poverty, 7, 11, 12–15, 30
    estimated cost to eliminate, 17

S

sanitation, 8, 11, 14, 17, 35
sea levels, 37–39, 42
slums, 20
sustainable development
    definition of, 6
    history of, 4–9

U

United Nations, 5–6, 8, 10, 17,
    33, 36
U.N. conferences, 5–7

ABOUT THE AUTHOR

Adam Winters has a liberal arts degree from the University of Texas in Austin. A nature lover and concerned environmentalist, he lives with his family on a small farm in central Texas, where he raises cattle and organic vegetables and contributes as a writer to various publications throughout Canada and the United States.

PHOTO CREDITS

Designer: Thomas Forget; Editor: Liz Gavril
Photo Researcher: Hillary Arnold